# Olive, the Orphan Reindeer

by
Michael Christie

with illustrations by
Margeaux Lucas

New Canaan Publishing Company Inc., New Canaan,
Connecticut

10 9 8 7 6 5 4 3 2 1

ISBN 1-889658-16-2

Printed in the United States of America by New Canaan Publishing Company Inc.

Library of Congress Cataloging-in-Publication Data

Christie, Michael, 1938-
    Olive, the orphan reindeer / by Michael Christie
        p.cm.
    Summary: Olive, an orphan reindeer who lives at the North Pole, enjoys helping get the presents ready for Christmas Eve but dreams of joining the team of deer pulling Santa's sleigh on the Big Trip.
    ISBN 1-889658-18-9 -- ISBN 1-889658-16-2 (trade paper)
    [1. Reindeer--Fiction. 2. Christmas--Fiction. 3. NorthPole--Fiction. 4. Santa Claus--Fiction.] I. Title.

PZ7.C4532 Ol 2000
[E]--dc21
                                                        99-088346

# Olive, the Orphan Reindeer

# 1. Wolves

The storm in the Barrens raged around the little reindeer with a nose like an olive.

"Mommy! Daddy!"

She'd lost her mother and father and brothers and sisters.

The night wind shrieked. The snowflakes stung her eyes.

"Mommy! Daddy! Where are you?"

But no one could hear her.

And now – *danger* – wolves!

She could smell them. They were close. Maybe they got my family, she thought, and want me too.

So the little reindeer ran as fast as she could.

In the fierce storm, she didn't know where she was going. She just knew she had to get away.

The wolves chased her, but she soon left them far behind. Even when she no longer picked up their scent, she ran and ran.

Finally, she came to the North Pole.

# 2. Santa And Mrs. Claus

Gasping for breath, Olive found herself in front of Santa and Mrs. Claus's house. The night here was calm and peaceful. She saw the two arm-in-arm on their door-step. They were look-ing at the stars.

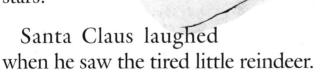

Santa Claus laughed when he saw the tired little reindeer.

"Ho! Ho! Ho! Look, my dear. A reindeer

with an olive for a nose! Goodness! Welcome to the North Pole, little one."

Mrs. Claus smiled. "Well, aren't you just the cutest thing though! We'll have to call you

Olive. Right, Santa?" Santa nodded.

"Do you like cookies, Olive?" Mrs. Claus asked.

"I don't know, ma'am," Olive said.

"Well, try this," Mrs. Claus said. Bringing Olive inside, she gave the reindeer a cookie. "It's raisin and oatmeal, fresh from my bakery."

Olive found it tasty. While she nibbled on it, Mrs. Claus tied a blue bow on Olive's head.

"There, Olive!" Mrs. Claus said, giving her a big hug. "You just needed a mite sprucing up."

"I hope you can stay a while, Olive," said Santa.

Olive felt there was little chance she'd see her family again, so she decided to make the North Pole her home.

# 3. Olive's Jobs

As the years passed and Olive got bigger, she became one of the best skaters among the spare reindeer. She always won the friendly races against them at Candy Cane Pond.

Olive also had important jobs to do during the Christmas season.

She hauled boxes of presents to Santa Claus's sleigh on the runway.

She delivered muffins from Mrs. Claus's bakery to the hospital.

She looked through the magic telescope to see which boys and girls were naughty or nice, and she reported their names to Number One, the chief elf.

In the toy factory, she checked for broken toys coming off a line in Quality Control.

She liked these jobs, but the job Olive wanted more than anything was to be on Santa's team. Will I be picked some day? she wondered.

# 4. A Foolish Dream

It was Christmas Eve again. As always, Olive wished she could go on the Big Trip. Many of her spare reindeer pals had gone. Why not me? she thought. But maybe that was a foolish dream.

Only this morning an elf had shouted, "You over there - no, not you, Jingles - the other reindeer. Yes, you, pimento nose. Give us some help."

But at dusk when Olive got off shift, she began to do some serious thinking. Maybe it wasn't a foolish dream at all. What did that smart alec elf know anyway?

So she decided right then to visit Santa and ask him if she could join the team.

# 5. A Meeting With Santa

As she stood in front of Santa's house, Olive wasn't so sure of herself.

"Just who do you think you are?" she said. But she'd come this far, so what did she have to lose? All Santa could do was say no. She hesitated, then she tapped at Santa's door.

She waited. No answer.

She tapped again.

No one was home.

She sighed. "Oh, well, I tried."

Just as Olive was about to leave, the door burst open.

"Ho! Ho! Ho! Well, well, look who it is!" Santa said. He had only one boot on. "I'm just getting ready to go over to Mission Control

to check things out before the Big Trip. What can I do for you, Olive?"

"Hi, Santa. I thought I'd ask if there, uh, was...was..."

"Was what, Olive?"

"Well...anything I could do."

Santa thought. "No, I can't think of any-thing."

"Oh."

"What did you have in mind?"

"Well, uh, well..." Olive was tongue-tied.

"Please, I'm really in a hurry," Santa said. "Well?"

When he hears what I want, he'll laugh at me, Olive thought. That's worse than a simple "no". She just blinked.

"I can't think of a thing you could do," Santa said.

"Well, I just thought I'd, you know, ask anyway."

Santa shrugged. "Thank you for asking, Olive."

"You're welcome, Santa."

She left. Santa scratched his head.

"What a strange conversation," he muttered.

# 6. Countdown

Take-off time was ninety-seven minutes away.

Best to forget about the Big Trip by keeping busy, Olive felt. Maybe Mrs. Claus wanted some muffins taken to the hospital.

Olive headed for the bakery. Magnificent smells drifted from it: mincemeat tarts, chocolate cakes, jelly doughnuts, date squares, brownies, buns, bread, all kinds of muffins, and cookies.

"Hi, Olive. That nose of yours sure works mighty fine," Mrs. Claus said. "Here's a nice warm raisin and oatmeal cookie, just for you."

16

"No, thank you, Mrs. Claus," Olive said. "I'm not hungry. I just came over to see if you wanted some muffins taken over to the hospital."

"I'm sorry, Olive. We made the muffin delivery this afternoon when you were at the toy factory."

"Oh."

Mrs. Claus gave Olive a close look. "What's the matter, Olive? Why the glum looking face?"

Olive pawed at the ground. "Well...it's nothing. Nothing."

Mrs. Claus fixed Olive's blue bow. It was crooked. "Something is bothering you. Tell me,

Olive, don't be shy with me. We girls have to stick together. What is it?"

"It's nothing, Mrs. Claus. I'd better go now and see if they need me one last time at the toy factory."

Olive trotted off.

"You're my favorite reindeer, you know. I'm always around if you need me," Mrs. Claus called after her.

# 7. Too Late

At the toy factory, Olive's best friend, Boomer, the chubby harness elf, sat on a crate by the shipping dock. He munched on a peanut butter sandwich.

*"Hi, Olive!"* Boomer shouted. He liked to shout rather than talk.

"Hi, Boomer. Do they need any more help inside?"

"Not now. They're just tying up some loose ends. We're ready."

"Oh." Olive wasn't needed here either.

"What's eating you, Olive? *Huh?* You look really sad."

"Well, it's just that I'd love to go on the Big Trip," Olive said.

"*Hey, come on!* You'll make it one day!"

"Oh, I don't know about that, Boomer."

"You *will*. You're *fast*. You always win the races on Candy Cane Pond. And you're *strong* too."

"I'm just a nobody. After all these years, I'm still called the *other* reindeer."

"*Aw, come on!* Mrs. Claus for one doesn't call you that," Boomer said. "Tell *her* what you want."

"Mrs. Claus doesn't do the hiring."

"No, but I'm sure she's got *some* clout with

20

Santa."

"I just talked to Mrs. Claus, and I couldn't tell her about...about my dream. I just couldn't."

"*Huh?* Why not?"

"Well, I..."

Boomer waved his sandwich in the air. "*Sweet potaters, Olive!* You can't just wait for something to happen. And that's what you're doing."

"I know, Boomer, I know." Olive wouldn't mention her visit with Santa Claus, or Boomer would get really steamed. "But I just don't like to be...pushy."

Boomer snorted. "*Pushy?* You really tick me off sometimes. You know that? The squeaky wheel gets the grease. Things won't come to you. And..."

"And what, Boomer?"

Boomer stared at his sandwich. "The Big Trip is only *eighty-nine minutes away.* But I have to say you can forget it just like the other ones. *It's too late.*"

Olive gulped. Maybe I should have said something to Mrs. Claus, she thought. I'll be staying behind again.

# 8. The Numbers Aren't Good

Meanwhile, Santa Claus, Number One, the chief elf, and Chip, the computer ace, were going over a few things in the Planning Room at Mission Control.

They studied a wall map. Mittens, Santa's orange cat, was on Santa's shoulders. Even he seemed interested in the map.

"Santa, the numbers aren't good," Chip said.

23

"We have a record number of kids this year, and we just don't have enough reindeer power."

Santa chuckled. "Chip, you worry too much. I have a great team, but we can always add one or two of the spare reindeer."

Mrs. Claus passed by. She cupped her ear to listen.

"One or two won't do it, Santa, even if we had them," Number One said. "Dr. Winters called me just before you arrived. An odd thing. The spare reindeer are in the hospital sick."

Santa gasped. "Oh, dear! All of them at once? That's terrible!"

"And the sleigh is loaded to overflowing," Chip said. "If we added any more toys, we couldn't lift off. Lots of toys have to be left

24

behind." He looked at his calculator. "The numbers aren't good."

"They certainly aren't, Chip," Santa said.

"Many places must be missed." Chip pointed at the map with a baseball bat. "Here, here, and here. And there."

Santa Claus sank into an armchair with his head in his hands. Mittens hid.

"But we can't let down any children," Santa moaned. "We can't! You're the computer expert, Chip. Think of something. Anything! We leave in fifty-six minutes. There must be something we can do."

Chip threw up his hands. "There isn't, Santa, and that's a fact."

After she heard this, Mrs. Claus hurried over to the hospital.

# 9. Blackmail

In the hospital ward, the spare reindeer lay in beds. With thermometers in their mouths were Speedy, Jingles, Flash, Igloo, Spinner, Rascal, Bingo, and Pokey.

Dr. Winters took out the thermometers and read them. "Hmmm," he said. "I can't see anything the matter with any of you." He looked at his watch. "It's Christmas Eve, with forty-three minutes until take-off. What if Santa needs some of you? Then what?"

"Then that'll be too bad," Pokey stated. "We're not going back to that gloomy old stable."

"Not until somebody paints it," said Flash.

"Hah! So that's it," Dr. Winters said. "Black-mail!"

"That's a mean thing to say," said Bingo. "But we're not going back to that stable. So there!"

"Get up! Get up!" Dr. Winters yelled. "Where's your pride? Where's your courage? Where's your loyalty? Get up! Immediately! This is nonsense! This is...uh, *please*. With jam on it. Well?"

But the reindeer just snuggled in their beds and answered with snores. They weren't going anywhere.

# 10. Not A Very Nice Idea

Mrs. Claus rushed into the ward. She was alarmed by what she saw.

"What's going on, Doctor?"

Dr. Winters shook his head. "I never thought I'd hear myself say this, Mrs. Claus. Never in a million years. But what we've got here is a bunch of fakers who want to sleep all day long in nice comfy beds. In short, they're on strike!"

Mrs. Claus thought. "I think I've got an idea. It's not a very nice one, but..."

She whispered into Dr. Winters' ear. The

reindeer squinted at them. What were they up to?

The doctor held up a needle. He gave it a squirt. The reindeer stirred.

"Now this might smart a little, you reindeer, but it's for your own good," Dr. Winters said.

The reindeer shot up in bed.

"Don't be scared," Dr. Winters said. "It'll only take a second."

"I feel a lot better, Dr. Winters," Jingles said.

"M-m-me too," Pokey stuttered.

"See you, Dr. Winters," said Igloo, bolting for the door.

"Don't call us, we'll call you," said the rest as they clomped after Igloo.

Mrs. Claus and Dr. Winters split their sides as the reindeer stampeded down the corridor.

# 11. Take-Off

Take-off was seconds away.

From the runway red, gold, green, and blue fireworks lit the North Pole sky with fantastic patterns.

 Two elves at the front of the sleigh blew a trumpet fanfare.

*Tah-tah tah tah-tah tah tah. Tah-Tah.*

Boomer sprinkled Santa's reindeer from his bag of magic sparkles. The sparkles gave the reindeer the power to fly.

Chip and Number One looked on with frowns. Everyone was nervous except for the reindeer.

"I'm all set, chief," said Dasher, and he pawed at the ground.

"Me too," said Dancer, and he shook his bells.

"Let's go, Santa," said Comet.

From the front of Santa's team came a red glow and a giggle.

The reindeer loved Christmas Eve. Santa

didn't have the heart to tell them thousands of children would be given a miss on this one.

He slumped in his sleigh. Even his beard seemed to droop.

Olive watched from a rise. Although she wanted to forget about the Big Trip, she just couldn't help coming to see the show. She especially loved the fireworks.

She heard the reindeer's excited voices. Oh, how she wished she could be one of them. But I'll always be left behind, she thought.

Olive turned away. She'd seen enough. A tear trickled down her cheek.

Suddenly there were cries of alarm. And...

# BANG!

# 12. What Boomer Did

The sleigh had crashed. Santa Claus was tossed into a snowbank. The reindeer sprawled on the runway. Boxes of presents were scattered everywhere. Olive galloped to the overturned sleigh. Boomer stood near it.

"Oh, no! This is awful! A disaster!" Olive cried. "What happened, Boomer?"

Boomer grinned. "I overloaded the sleigh when nobody was looking. *I put a set of barbells across the back of the runners.*"

"What! But why?"

*"You want to go with them, don't you?"*

"Shh! Of course I want to go, but..."

"Well, if the team can't get airborne then you're in. *You're in!*"

"But...but..."

"Oh-oh!" Boomer clasped his mouth. "Look who's coming."

# 13. No Time To Lose

Number One marched toward them. His face was red with anger.

"I heard all that, Boomer. Oh, Santa! Santa!" he called. "I think there is something you should know."

Santa struggled to his feet and brushed snow off himself.

"What's going on here?" Santa said.

"Tell Santa Claus the disgraceful thing you did, Boomer," Number One ordered. "Go on."

Boomer hung his head. "I overloaded the

sleigh with some barbells. I'm sorry, Santa, I really am. But please forget what I did, and give Olive a chance to go with you. That's why I did it. Olive is as fast as *greased lightning*."

Santa shook his head. The accident had confused him.

"Olive?" he said. "Olive?" Then it dawned. "Yes, Olive! I was just talking to you. So you want to help deliver the presents, do you, Olive?"

"Oh, yes, Santa. That's really why I came to see you."

Boomer gave Olive a surprised look. "*Huh? You did?*"

Santa stroked his beard. "So that was it! But why didn't you say so? Oh, never mind. We've got no time to lose. Come along, Olive."

But Olive didn't move. "I'd love to, Santa, but I don't think it would be fair to go after all this. If not for Boomer, you'd all be in the sky by now."

Boomer clenched his teeth. "Olive, you're going to blow it."

"Hmm, I see," Santa said. "I see."

For a while no one knew what to say. Finally, Number One spoke up. He'd cooled off.

"Santa, may I say something?" he said. "Although I do not approve of such a deed, I think Boomer is a good fellow. He has served us well for many years. Perhaps we can overlook what he did."

Santa nodded. "I agree, Number One. Everybody is entitled to a mistake. We'll give Boomer a second chance. So, Olive? Do you want to come? Yes or no?"

Olive could hardly believe it. Was her dream about to come true?

"Whoopee!" she shouted. "You'll see I'm really fast and strong, Santa."

Santa's eyes twinkled. He patted Olive on the head.

"Don't worry, Olive," Santa said. "I've had my eye on you, and I know how fast and strong you are. You were going to be on the team sooner or later. So as of now, you're officially hired."

Chip joined them. He was studying his calculator and he didn't look happy. "I hate to be a party pooper, Santa, but this won't change much," he said. "With the help of Olive, we can make Los Angeles just before sun up. But many other places will still get left out."

Santa sighed. "I know, I know, I hadn't forgotten, Chip. How could I? All those children will be heart-broken. They'll never forgive me. But there's nothing we can do."

# 14. Mrs. Claus's Surprise

At that moment they heard a whistle in the distance. It came from Mrs. Claus. She wore a red-and-white Santa outfit. And she was driving a team made up of the eight spare reindeer.

"Hee-hah! Giddy-up, my honeys!" Mrs. Claus urged. The spare reindeer looked as fit as ever. They came at full steam. Snow swirled around their pounding hooves.

Santa's mouth fell open as Mrs. Claus pulled up beside him.

"Mrs. Claus! Goodness! What a surprise!" Santa said. "What are you doing here?"

"Well, dear, I heard you had a problem," Mrs. Claus said.

"We do, we do. A whopper. But I thought all the spare reindeer were in the hospital."

Mrs. Claus smiled. "They were. Flat on their backs, until Dr. Winters came up with a...a cure, you might say. And then I did a little wheeling and dealing, to get their stable a new paint job. You really should see it, dear."

"We can talk about that later, my dear. But right now, I'd like to know why you're here."

"Well, I thought we could load up my sleigh and I'll go with you. If you don't mind."

Santa clapped his hands. "Mind? Why should I mind? That's a terrific idea! You really want to go, don't you, my dear?"

"It will be a hoot. A real hoot."

"All these years, and you've never once said anything."

"Well, wouldn't a passenger have made the sleigh too heavy?" Mrs. Claus said. "So? What do you say?"

# 15. The Big Trip

Santa turned to Boomer.

"Quick, Boomer! Hitch up Olive to Mrs. Claus's team. That will give us nine reindeer each."

Boomer saluted. *"Right away, Santa!"* Boomer hitched Olive in the lead.

A dozen elves gathered up the scattered toys. Another dozen brought the ones left over in the toy factory. The sleighs were quickly loaded.

Boomer sprinkled Mrs. Claus's reindeer with the magic sparkles. For a moment, the reindeer rose and floated on air. Mrs. Claus's team was now ready to fly.

"Up and at 'em, Olive!" whooped Mrs. Claus. "Ho-ho! Ho-ho!"

Santa winked. "You've got the words, my dear, but, well, the tune needs some work."

Then with a merry "Ho! Ho! Ho!" and a "Ho-ho! Ho-ho!" Santa and Mrs. Claus whooshed off into the twinkling stars and over the moon.

The elves jumped up and down and cheered

the two sleighs in the sky. "Yippee! Yippee!" A few toasted each other with mugs of hot chocolate.

As she led Mrs. Claus's team, Olive held her head up high.

All the boys and girls got their presents on time and they were delighted.

So was Olive. And she did such a super job that from then on she made the Big Trip with Mrs. Claus every Christmas Eve.